'If I stopped now,
after coming all
this way – well,
they'd call me
an idiot!'

LEO TOLSTOY
Born 1828, Yasnaya Polyana, Russian Empire
Died 1910, Astapovo, Russian Empire

'How Much Land Does A Man Need?' and 'What Men Live By',
published in their original Russian in 1836 and 1835 respectively.
They are taken from *How Much Land Does a Man Need? and
Other Stories.*

LEO TOLSTOY

How Much Land Does A Man Need?

Translated by
Ronald Wilks

PENGUIN BOOKS

PENGUIN CLASSICS

UK | USA | Canada | Ireland | Australia
India | New Zealand | South Africa

Penguin Books is part of the Penguin Random House group of companies
whose addresses can be found at global.penguinrandomhouse.com.

Penguin
Random House
UK

This edition published in Penguin Classics 2015
003

Translation copyright © Ronald Wilks, 1993

The moral right of the translator has been asserted

Set in 9/12.4 pt Baskerville 10 Pro
Typeset by Jouve (UK), Milton Keynes
Printed in Great Britain by Clays Ltd, St Ives plc

A CIP catalogue record for this book is available from the British Library

ISBN: 978-0-141-39774-0

www.greenpenguin.co.uk

Contents

How Much Land Does A Man Need?

1

An elder sister came from the town to visit her younger sister in the country. This elder sister was married to a merchant and the younger to a peasant in the village. The two sisters sat down for a talk over a cup of tea and the elder started boasting about the superiority of town life, with all its comforts, the fine clothes her children wore, the exquisite food and drink, the skating, parties and visits to the theatre.

The younger sister resented this and in turn scoffed at the life of a merchant's wife and sang the praises of her own life as a peasant.

'I wouldn't care to change my life for yours,' she said. 'I admit mine is dull, but at least we have no worries. You live in grander style, but you must do a great deal of business or you'll be ruined. You know the proverb, "Loss is Gain's elder brother." One day you are rich and the next you might find yourself out in the street. Here in the country we don't have those ups and downs. A peasant's life may be poor, but it's long. Although we may never be rich, we'll always have enough to eat.'

Then the elder sister said her piece.

'Enough to eat indeed with nothing but those filthy pigs and calves! What do you know about nice clothes and good manners! However hard your good husband slaves away you'll spend your lives in the muck and that's where you'll die. And the same goes for your children.'

'Well, what of it?' the younger sister retorted. 'That's how it is here. But at least we know where we are. We don't have to crawl to anyone and we're afraid of no one. But you in the town are surrounded by temptations. All may be well one day, the next the Devil comes along and tempts your husband with cards, women and drink. And then you're ruined. It does happen, doesn't it?'

Pakhom, the younger sister's husband, was lying over the stove listening to the women's chatter.

'It's true what you say,' he said. 'Take me. Ever since I was a youngster I've been too busy tilling the soil to let that kind of nonsense enter my head. My only grievance is that I don't have enough land. Give me enough of that and I'd fear no one – not even the Devil himself!'

The sisters finished their tea, talked a little longer about dresses, cleared away the tea things and went to bed.

But the Devil had been sitting behind the stove and had heard everything. He was delighted that a peasant's wife had led her husband to boast that if he had enough land he would fear no one, not even the Devil. 'Good!' he thought. 'I'll have a little game with you. I shall see that you have plenty of land and that way I'll get you in my clutches!'

2

Not far from the village lived a lady with a small estate of about three hundred acres. She had always been on good terms with the peasants and had never ill-treated them. But then she had taken on an old soldier to manage her estate and he proceeded to harass the peasants by constantly imposing fines. No matter how careful Pakhom was, one of his horses might stray into the lady's oats, or a cow might sometimes wander into her garden, or some calves might venture out on to her meadows. Every time this happened he would have to pay a fine.

Pakhom would pay up and then he would go and swear at his family and beat them. All that summer Pakhom had to put up with a great deal from that manager, so he welcomed winter when it came and his cattle had to be kept in the shed: although he begrudged the fodder, at least he wouldn't have to worry about them straying.

That winter word got round that the lady wanted to sell some of her land and that the innkeeper on the highway was trying to agree on a price with her. The peasants took this news very badly. 'If that innkeeper gets his hands on that land he'll start slapping even more fines on us than that manager. But we can't survive without it, we all depend on it for our living.'

So a few peasants, in the name of the village commune, begged the lady not to sell any of her land to the innkeeper and to let them buy it, offering her a better price. The lady agreed. Then the members of the commune thought of buying the whole estate. They met once, they met twice, but no progress was made: the Devil had set them at loggerheads and there was nothing they could agree upon. In the end they decided to buy the land in separate lots, each according to what he could afford. The lady agreed to this as well.

One day Pakhom learned that one of his neighbours was buying about fifty acres and that the lady had taken half payment in cash, allowing the man one year to pay the balance. This made Pakhom very envious. 'They'll buy up all the land,' he thought, 'and I'll be left with nothing.' So he conferred with his wife.

'Everyone's buying land,' he said. 'We must get hold of twenty acres, or thereabouts. If we don't we won't be able to live, what with that manager bleeding us white with fines.'

So they racked their brains as to how they could buy some of the land. They had a hundred roubles saved up, so that by selling a foal and half their bees, by sending one of their sons out to work for someone who paid wages in advance and borrowing from a brother-in-law, they managed to scrape together half the money.

Then Pakhom took the money, chose about thirty acres of partly wooded land and went off to the lady to see if he could strike a deal. He managed to get the thirty acres, they shook hands on it and Pakhom paid a deposit. Then they went into town and signed the deeds, Pakhom paying half cash down and pledging to settle the balance within two years.

And so Pakhom now had land. He borrowed money for seeds and sowed the newly bought land; the harvest was excellent. Within a year he had repaid both the lady and his brother-in-law. Now he was a landowner, in the full sense of the word: he ploughed and sowed his own fields, reaped his own hay, cut his own timber and could pasture his cattle on his own land. Whenever he rode out to plough the land which was now his for ever, or to inspect his young corn and meadows, he was filled with joy. He felt that the grass that grew and the flowers that bloomed were different from any other grass and flowers. Before, when he had ridden over that land, it had seemed the same as any other. But now it was something quite special.

3

So Pakhom lived a landowner's life and he was happy. And in fact all would have been well had other peasants not trespassed on his cornfields and meadows. He spoke to them very politely, but they took no notice. Herdsmen let their cows stray on to his meadows, then horses wandered into his corn on their way home from night pasture. Again and again Pakhom drove them out without taking further action, but in the end he lost patience and complained to the District Court. He knew very well that the peasants weren't doing it deliberately but because they were short of land. But still he thought, 'I can't let this go on. Before long they'll have destroyed all I have. I must teach them a lesson.'

So he taught them a lesson in court, then another, making several of them pay fines. Pakhom's neighbours resented this and once again began to let their cattle stray on his land, this time on purpose. One night someone managed to get into Pakhom's wood and felled about ten young lime-trees for their bark. Next day, when Pakhom was riding through his wood, he suddenly noticed something white on the ground. He went nearer and saw tree-trunks lying all around, stripped of their bark, with the stumps lying nearby. 'If he'd only just cut one or two down, but that devil's left me with one tree standing and cleared the rest.' Pakhom seethed with anger. 'Oh, if I knew who did it I'd show him a thing or two!' For a long time he racked his brains and finally concluded, 'It must be Semyon, it can't be anyone else.' So off he went to search Semyon's place, but he found nothing and all the two men did was swear at each other. Pakhom was more convinced than ever that it was Semyon's work and he lodged a complaint. The magistrates sat for ages debating the case and finally acquitted Semyon for lack of evidence. This incensed Pakhom even more and he had a stormy session with the village elder and the magistrates.

'You are hand in glove with thieves,' he protested. 'If you were honest men you wouldn't let a thief like him off the hook.'

As a result Pakhom fell out with the magistrates as well as his neighbours, who threatened to burn his cottage down.

And so, although Pakhom had plenty of leg-room now, he felt that the commune was hemming him in.

Around that time rumours were in the air that many peasants were leaving to settle in new parts of the country. Pakhom thought, '*I* don't really need to go away, what with all that land of mine. But if some of the villagers were to go there'd be more room for others. I could buy their land and make my estate bigger. Life would be easier then, but as things are, it's still too cramped here for my liking.'

One day a peasant who was passing through stopped at Pakhom's cottage. They let him stay the night and gave him food. Pakhom asked where he was from and the man replied that he had come from the south, from the other side of the Volga, where he had been working. Then he told how people from his own village had settled there, joined the commune and had been allotted twenty-five acres each. 'The land is so fertile,' he said, 'that rye grows as high as a horse and it's so thick you can make a whole sheaf from only five handfuls! One peasant arrived with a copeck and only his bare hands to work with and now he has six horses and two cows.'

Pakhom was terribly excited by this news. 'Why should I have to scrape a living cooped up here,' he thought, 'when I could be leading a good life somewhere else? I could sell the land and cottage and with the money I'd be able to build myself a house there and start a whole new farm. But here there's no room to breathe and I get nothing but aggravation. I must go and find out what it's like for myself.'

When summer came he was ready and he set off. He went down the Volga to Samara by steamboat, then walked the remaining three hundred miles to the new settlement, which was just as the visitor had described. All the men had plenty of space, each having been allotted twenty-five acres without charge and welcomed into the commune. Anyone who had the money could also buy as much of the finest freehold land as he wanted, at three roubles an acre – there was no limit!

Towards autumn, after finding out all he needed to know, Pakhom went home and started selling up. He sold the land at a profit, his home and all his cattle, resigned from the commune and waited until the spring, when he left with his family for the new settlement.

4

When he arrived with his family Pakhom managed to get himself on the register of a large village commune, having duly moistened the elders' throats. All was signed and sealed and Pakhom was granted a hundred acres (twenty for each member of his family, in different fields), besides the use of the communal pasture. Then he put up some buildings and stocked his farm with cattle. The allotted land alone was three times as much as at home and it was perfect for growing corn. He was ten times better off here, for he had plenty of arable land and pasturage, and he was able to keep as many cattle as he wanted.

At first, while he was busy building and stocking up, everything seemed wonderful. But no sooner had he settled down to his new life than he began to feel cramped even here. During the first year he had sowed wheat on the allotted land and the crop had been excellent. But when he wanted to sow more wheat he found he needed more land: the other land he had been allotted was not suitable for wheat. In the south wheat is sown only on grass or on fallow land. They sow it for one or two years and then leave it fallow until the land is overgrown with feather-grass again. This type of land was in great demand and there wasn't enough to go round, so that people quarrelled over it. The richer ones sowed their own, whilst the poorer ones had to mortgage theirs to merchants to pay their taxes. Pakhom wanted to sow more wheat, so the following year he rented some fields from a dealer for one year. He sowed a great deal of wheat and had a good crop. But the fields were a long way from the village and the wheat had to be carted more than ten miles. Then Pakhom noticed that some peasant farmers with large homesteads in the neighbourhood were becoming very wealthy. 'What if I bought some freehold land and built myself a homestead like theirs?' he wondered. 'Then everything would be within easy reach.' And he tried to think how he could buy some.

Pakhom farmed the same way for three years, renting land and sowing wheat. They were good years, the crops were good and he was able to save some money. But Pakhom grew tired of having to rent land, year after year, of having to waste his time scrambling after it. Whenever good land came up for sale the peasants would immediately fall over themselves to buy it and it would all be gone before he could do anything: he was never quick enough and so he had no land for sowing his wheat. So in the third year he went halves with a merchant in buying a plot of pasture land outright from some peasants. They had already ploughed it when someone sued the peasants over it and as a result all their work was wasted. 'If it had been *my* land,' Pakhom thought, 'I wouldn't have been under an obligation to anyone and I wouldn't have got into that mess.'

So Pakhom tried to discover where to buy some freehold land. He came across a peasant who, having purchased some thirteen hundred acres, had then gone bankrupt and was selling the land off very cheaply. Pakhom bargained with

9

him. After much haggling they finally agreed upon fifteen hundred roubles, half cash down, half to be paid at a later date. The deal was all but signed and sealed when a passing merchant called at Pakhom's to have his horses fed. They drank tea together and got into conversation. The merchant said that he was on his way back from the far-off land of the Bashkirs, where he had bought some thirteen thousand acres for a mere thousand roubles. When Pakhom questioned him further the merchant told him, 'All I had to do was give the old men there a few presents – a hundred roubles' worth of silk robes and carpets, a chest of tea, and vodka for anyone who wanted it. I managed to get the land for twenty copecks an acre.' He showed Pakhom the title deeds. 'The land is near a river and it's all beautiful grassy steppe.'

Pakhom continued to ply him with questions.

'There's so much land that you couldn't walk round it all in a year. It all belongs to the Bashkirs. Yes, the people there are as stupid as sheep and you can get land off them for practically nothing.'

'Well,' Pakhom thought, 'why should I pay a thousand roubles for thirteen hundred acres and saddle myself with debt? To think what I could buy with the same money down there!'

5

Pakhom asked him how to get there and as soon as he had said goodbye to the merchant he prepared to leave. He left his wife behind and set off, taking a workman with him. First they stopped off in town and bought a chest of tea, vodka and other presents, just as the old merchant had advised. Then they travelled for miles and miles until, on the seventh day, they reached the Bashkir settlement. Everything was as the merchant had described: the people lived on the steppe, near a river, in tents of thick felt. They neither ploughed the soil nor ate bread, and their cattle and horses wandered in herds over the steppe. The foals were tethered behind the tents and the mares brought over to them twice a day. These mares were milked and from the milk kumiss was made. The women also made cheese from the kumiss and all the men seemed concerned with was drinking kumiss and tea, eating mutton and playing their pipes. All of them were cheerful and well-fed, and they spent the whole summer idling about. The Bashkirs were very ignorant, knew no Russian, but were kindly people.

The moment they spotted Pakhom, the Bashkirs streamed out of their tents and surrounded their visitor. An interpreter was found and Pakhom told him that he had come about some land. The Bashkirs were delighted and took Pakhom off to one of the finest tents, where they made him sit on some rugs piled with cushions, while they formed a circle and offered him tea and kumiss. Then they slaughtered a sheep and fed him with mutton. Pakhom fetched the presents from his cart, handed them round and shared the tea out. The Bashkirs were delighted. For a while they talked away amongst themselves and then told the interpreter to translate.

'They want me to tell you,' the interpreter said, 'that they've taken a great liking to you and that it's our custom to do all we can to please a guest and repay him for his gifts. You have given us presents, so please tell us if there is anything of ours that you would like so we can show our gratitude.'

'What I like most of all here,' Pakhom replied, 'is your land. Back home there isn't enough to go round and, what's more, the soil is exhausted. But here you have plenty and it looks very good. I've never seen soil like it.'

The interpreter translated and then the Bashkirs went into a lengthy conference. Although Pakhom did not understand, he could see how cheerful they were, laughing and shouting. Then they all became quiet, glanced at Pakhom and the interpreter continued, 'I'm to tell you that they would be only too pleased to let you have as much land as you like in return for your kindness. All you have to do is point it out and it will be yours.'

Then they conferred again and started arguing about something. Pakhom asked what it was and the interpreter told him, 'Some of them are saying they should first consult the elder about the land. They can't do anything without his permission, but some of the others say it's not necessary.'

6

While the Bashkirs were arguing, a man in a fox-fur cap suddenly came into the tent, whereupon they all became quiet and stood up.

'It's the elder,' the interpreter explained.

Pakhom immediately fetched his best robe and presented it with five pounds of tea to the elder, who accepted the gifts and then sat in the place of honour. The Bashkirs immediately started telling him something. After listening for a while the elder motioned with his head for them to be quiet and then spoke to Pakhom in Russian.

'Well now,' he said. 'It's all right. Choose whatever land you like, there's plenty of it.'

'How can I just go and take whatever I like?' Pakhom wondered. 'I must have it all signed and sealed somehow. Now they tell me it's mine, but who knows, they might change their minds?' So he told them, 'Thank you for your kind words. Yes, you do have a great deal of land, but I need only a little. However, I would like to be sure which will be mine, so couldn't it be measured and made over to me by some sort of contract? Our lives are in God's hands and although you good people are willing to give me the land now, it's possible your children might want it back again.'

'What you say is true,' said the elder. 'We can have a contract drawn up.'

Pakhom said, 'I've heard that you made some land over to a merchant not long ago, together with the title deeds. I would like you to do the same with me.'

The elder understood. 'That's no problem,' he said. 'We have a clerk here and we can ride into town and have the documents properly witnessed and signed.'

'But what about the price?' Pakhom asked.

'We have a set price – a thousand roubles a day.'

Pakhom did not understand.

'What kind of rate is that – a *day*? How many acres would that be?'

'We don't reckon your way. We sell by the day. However

much you can walk round in one day will be yours. And the price is a thousand roubles a day.'

Pakhom was amazed. 'Well, a man can walk round a lot of land in one day,' he said.

The elder burst out laughing. 'Well, all of it will be yours,' he replied. 'But there's one condition: if you don't return to your starting-point the same day, your money will be forfeited.'

'But how can I mark where I've been?'

'We'll all go to whatever place you select and wait until you've completed your circuit. You must take a spade, dig a hole at every turning and leave the turf piled up. Afterwards, we will go from hole to hole with a plough. You may make as large a circuit as you like, only you must be back at your starting-point by sunset. All the land you can walk round will be yours.'

Pakhom was absolutely delighted. An early start was decided on and after talking for a while they drank kumiss, ate some mutton and then had tea. This went on until night-fall. Then the Bashkirs made up a feather-bed for Pakhom and left. They promised to be ready to ride out to the chosen spot before sunrise.

7

Pakhom lay down on the feather-bed, but the thought of all that land kept him awake. 'Tomorrow,' he thought, 'I shall mark out a really large stretch. In one day I can easily walk thirty-five miles. The days are long now – just think how much land I'll have from walking that distance! I'll sell the poorer bits, or let it to the peasants. I'll take the best for myself and farm it. I'll have two ox-ploughs and hire a couple of labourers to work them. Yes, I'll cultivate about a hundred and fifty acres and let the cattle graze the rest.'

Pakhom did not sleep a wink that night and dozed off only just before dawn. The moment he fell asleep he had a dream: he seemed to be lying in the same tent and could hear some-one roaring with laughter outside. Wondering who was laughing like that he got up, went out and saw that same Bashkir elder sitting there, holding his sides and rolling about in fits of laughter. He went closer and asked, 'What are you laughing at?' And then he saw that it wasn't the elder at all, but the merchant who had called on him a few days before and told him about the land. And just as Pakhom asked him, 'Have you been here long?' the merchant turned into the peasant who had come up from the Volga and visited him at home. And then Pakhom saw that it wasn't the peas-ant, but the Devil himself, with horns and hoofs, sitting there laughing his head off, while before him lay a barefoot man wearing only shirt and trousers. When Pakhom took a closer look he saw that the man was dead and that it was himself. Pakhom woke up in a cold sweat. 'The things one dreams about!' he thought. Then he looked round and saw that it was getting light at the open door – dawn was breaking. 'I must go and wake them,' he thought, 'it's time to start.' So Pakhom got up, roused the workman, who was sleeping in the cart, ordered him to harness the horse and went off to wake the Bashkirs. 'It's time to go out on the steppe and measure the land,' he said. The Bashkirs got up, assembled, and then the elder came and joined them. They drank some more kumiss and offered Pakhom tea, but he was impatient to be off. 'If we're going,' he said, 'let's go. It's time.'

8

So the Bashkirs got ready and left, some on horses, others in carts. Pakhom went to his little cart with him. They came out on to the open steppe just as the sun was rising. They climbed a small hill (called a 'shikhan' in Bashkir). Then the Bashkirs got out of their carts, dismounted from their horses and gathered in one place. The elder went over to Pakhom and pointed.

'Look,' he said, 'that's all ours, as far as the eye can see. Choose any part you like.'

Pakhom's eyes lit up, for the land was all virgin soil, flat as the palm of one's hand, black as poppy-seed, with different kinds of grass growing breast-high in the hollows.

The elder took off his fox-fur cap and put it on the ground.

'Let this be the marker: this is the starting point to which you must return. All the land you can walk round will be yours.'

Pakhom took out his money, placed it on the cap, took off his outer coat, so that he was wearing only a sleeveless undercoat, tightened his belt below the waist and stuffed a small bag of bread inside his shirt. Then he tied a flask of water to the belt, pulled up his boots, took the spade from his workman and was ready to leave. He could not decide which direction to take at first as the land was so good everywhere. Then he decided, 'It's all good land, so I'll walk towards the sunrise.' He turned to the east, stretching himself as he waited for the sun to appear above the horizon. 'There's no point in wasting time,' he thought. 'And it's easier walking while it's still cool.' The moment the sun's rays came flooding over the horizon Pakhom put the spade on one shoulder and walked out on to the steppe.

Pakhom walked neither quickly nor slowly. When he had gone about three quarters of a mile he stopped, dug a hole and piled the pieces of turf high on top of each other so that they were easily visible. The stiffness had now gone from his legs and he lengthened his stride. A little further on he stopped again and dug another hole.

When Pakhom looked back he could see quite clearly the small hill tyres of the cart-wheels. Pakhom guessed that he had covered about three miles. He was beginning to feel warmer, so he tool off his undercoat, flung it over his shoulder and walked another three miles. It was hot, and a look at the sun reminded him it was time for breakfast.

'Well, that's the first stretch completed!' he thought. 'But there are four to a day and it's too early to start turning. I must take these boots off, though.'

So he sat down, took off his boots, stuck them behind his belt and moved on. The going was easy now and he thought. 'I'll do another three miles and then turn left. The land's so beautiful here, it would be a pity to miss out on any of it. The further I go, the better the land gets.' So for a while he carried straight on and when he looked back the hill was barely visible and the people on it looked like black ants; he could just glimpse something that glinted in the sun.

'Well,' thought Pakhom, 'I've walked enough in this direction, I should be turning now. Besides, I'm stewing in this heat and terribly thirsty.' So he stopped, dug a large hole, piled up the turf, untied his flask, drank and then turned sharp left. On and on he walked – the grass was higher here and it was very hot.

Pakhom began to feel tired. He glanced at the sun and saw that it was noon. 'Well,' he thought, 'I must have a little rest.' So he stopped, sat down and had some bread and water. He did not stretch out, though, thinking, 'Once I lie down I'll fall asleep.' After a few minutes he carried on. At first it was easy – the food had given him strength. But by now it was extremely hot and he began to feel sleepy. Still, he kept going and thought of the proverb, 'A moment's pain can be a lifetime's gain.'

He had walked a long way in the same direction and was just about to turn left when he spotted a lush hollow and decided it would be a pity to lose it. 'What a good place for growing flax!' he thought. So he carried straight on until he had walked right round the low-lying meadows, dug a hole the other side, and then he turned the second corner. Pakhom looked back at the hill: it was shimmering in the heat and through the haze it was difficult to see all the people there – they were at least ten miles away. 'Well,' thought Pakhom, 'I've made those sides too long, this one has to be shorter.' So he started the third side, quickening his step. He looked at the sun and saw that it was already half way to the horizon, but he had completed only about one mile of the third side. The starting-point was still ten miles away. 'No,' he thought, 'although it will make the land a bit lopsided I must take the shortest way back. It's no good trying to grab too much, I've quite enough already!'

Pakhom hastily dug another hole and headed straight for the hill.

9

On the way back Pakhom found the going tough. The heat had exhausted him, his bare feet were cut and bruised and his legs were giving way. He wanted to rest, but this was out of the question – he would never get back by sunset. The sun waits for no man and was sinking lower and lower. 'Oh,' he wondered, 'have I blundered, trying to take too much? What if I'm not back in time?' He looked towards the hill, then at the sun. The hill was far off, the sun was close to the horizon.

But Pakhom struggled on. Although it was very hard, he walked faster and faster. On and on he went – but there was still a long way to go. He started running and threw away his coat, boots, flask, cap, keeping only the spade which he used for leaning on. 'Oh dear,' he thought, 'I've been too greedy. Now I've ruined it. I'll never get back by sunset.' His fear made him only more breathless. On he ran, his shirt soaking and his trousers clinging to him: his throat was parched. His lungs were working like a blacksmith's bellows, his heart beat like a hammer and his legs did not seem to be his – he felt that they were breaking . . . Pakhom was terrified and thought, 'All this strain will be the death of me.'

Although he feared death, he could not stop. 'If I stopped now, after coming all this way – well, they'd call me an idiot!' So on he ran until he was close enough to hear the Bashkirs yelling and cheering him on. Their shouts spurred him on all the more, so he summoned his last ounce of strength and kept running. But by now the sun was almost touching the horizon: veiled in mist, it was large and blood-red. It was about to set, but although it did not have very far to sink it was no distance to the starting-point either. Pakhom could see the people on the hill now, waving their arms and urging him on. He could see the fox-fur cap on the ground with the money on it; he could see the elder sitting there with his arms pressed to his sides. And Pakhom remembered his dream. 'I've plenty of land now, but will God let me live to enjoy it? No, I'm finished . . . I'll never make it.'

Pakhom looked at the sun – it had reached the earth now: half of its great disc had dipped below the horizon. With all the strength he had left Pakhom lurched forwards with his full weight, hardly able to move his legs quickly enough to stop himself falling. He reached the hill – and everything suddenly became dark. He looked round and saw that the sun had set. Pakhom groaned. 'All that effort has been in vain,' he thought. He wanted to stop, when he heard the Bashkirs still cheering him on and he realized that from where he was at the bottom of the hill the sun had apparently set, but not for those on top. Pakhom took a deep breath and rushed up the hill which was still bathed in sunlight. When he reached the top he saw his cap with the elder sitting by it, holding his sides and laughing his head off. Then he remembered the dream and he groaned. His legs gave way, he fell forward and managed to reach the cap with his hands.

'Oh, well done!' exclaimed the elder. 'That's a lot of land you've earned yourself!'

Pakhom's workman ran up and tried to lift his master, but the blood flowed from his mouth. Pakhom was dead.

The Bashkirs clicked their tongues sympathetically.

Pakhom's workman picked up the spade, dug a grave for his master – six feet from head to heel, which was exactly the right length – and buried him.

What Men Live By

We know that we have passed from death unto life, because we love the brethren. He that loveth not his brother abideth in death. (I John iii, 14)

But whoso hath this world's good, and seeth his brother have need, and shutteth up his bowels of compassion from him, how dwelleth the love of God in him? (I John iii, 17)

My little children, let us not love in word, neither in tongue: but in deed and in truth. (I John iii, 18)

. . . for love is of God; and every one that loveth is born of God, and knoweth God. (I John iv, 7)

He that loveth not knoweth not God; for God is love. (I John iv, 8)

No man hath seen God at any time. If we love one another, God dwelleth in us . . . (I John iv, 12)

God is love; and he that dwelleth in love dwelleth in God, and God in him. (I John iv, 16)

If a man say, I love God, and hateth his brother, he is a liar: for he that loveth not his brother whom he hath seen, how can he love God whom he hath not seen? (I John iv, 20)

1

Once there was a shoemaker who had neither house nor land of his own and who lived in a peasant's cottage with his wife and children, supporting them by what work he could get. Bread was expensive but his work was cheap and the little he earned was spent on food for his family. He and his wife had only one winter coat between them and even that was in a sorry state. For the past two years he had been saving to buy sheepskins for a new one.

By autumn he had scraped together a small sum: there was the three-rouble note that his wife kept in a little wooden box, as well as the five roubles and twenty copecks that some of the villagers owed him.

One morning he decided to go to the village to buy the skins. He put his wife's wadded twill jacket over his shirt and over that his own cloth coat. After breakfast he put the three-rouble note in his pocket, cut himself a walking-stick and set off.

'With the five roubles that one of them owes me,' he thought, 'plus the three I already have, I should have enough to buy the sheepskins.'

When he reached the village he stopped at a cottage, but the owner was out. His wife did not have the money, but she promised to send her husband over with it by the end of the week. So he called on another peasant who swore he was short of cash and that all he could manage was twenty copecks that were owing for some boot repairs. And then, when the shoemaker tried to buy the skins on credit, the dealer would not trust him.

'Bring me the money first,' he said. 'Then you can pick whatever skins you like. We all know how hard it is to collect what's owing to us!'

And so the shoemaker did no business that day, apart from twenty copecks for the repairs and a pair of felt boots that needed soling.

All this depressed the shoemaker and after spending the twenty copecks on vodka he set off for home without any skins. Earlier that morning he had felt a sharp nip in the air, but after a few vodkas he warmed up – even though he had no proper winter coat. As he walked down the road, striking frozen clods of earth with his stick in one hand and swinging the felt boots in the other, he started talking to himself.

'I feel quite warm without a coat,' he said. 'I've only had a drop, yet I can feel it rushing through every vein in my body. I don't need any sheepskins! I'm going home, with all my troubles behind me. That's the sort of man I am! Why should I worry? I can survive without a new coat – I won't need one for ages. Only, the wife won't be too happy. But it's really rotten when you do a job and the customer tries to string you along and doesn't pay up. You just wait – if you don't bring me the money I'll have the shirt off your back, I swear it! It's a bit much, what with a measly twenty copecks at a time. What can I do with twenty copecks? Spend it on drink, that's all. You say you're hard up. Well, what about me? You've a house, cattle, everything, but all I have is on my back. You grow your own corn, while I have to go out and buy mine. Whatever happens I must spend three roubles a week on bread alone. By the time I get home there won't be any left and I'll have to fork out another rouble and a half. So, you'd better pay up!'

The shoemaker kept rambling on like this until he drew near the wayside chapel at the bend in the road where something whitish just behind it caught his eye. But by now it was growing dark and although he strained his eyes he could not make out what it was. 'There wasn't any stone there before,' he thought. 'Perhaps it's a cow? No, it doesn't look like one at all. From the head it looks like a man and it's all white. But what would a man be doing there?'

He went a few steps closer and could now make it out quite clearly. How amazing! It *was* a man sitting there, but he could not see if he were dead or alive, and he was naked and quite motionless, his back propped against the chapel wall. The shoemaker was terrified and thought, 'A man's been murdered, stripped naked and dumped. If I go any nearer I might get mixed up in all sorts of troubles.'

And so the shoemaker went on his way. He walked behind the chapel to avoid having to look at him again. After a short distance he turned round and saw that the man was no longer leaning against the wall, but was moving, as if trying to see who he was. The shoemaker felt even more frightened and thought, 'Shall I go back or simply carry on? If I go back something terrible might happen. Who knows what kind of man he might be? I bet he's up to no good. Besides, he might suddenly jump to his feet and start choking the life out of me – and there'd be nothing I could do about it. And if he doesn't throttle me I might get lumbered with looking after him. But how can I help a naked man? I couldn't let him have the last shirt off my back. Please God, help me!'

And the shoemaker quickened his stride. He had almost left the chapel behind when his conscience began to prick him. He stopped in the middle of the road.

'How could you do such a thing, Semyon?' he reproached himself. 'That man might be dying miserably and you're such a coward you'd leave him there to die. Or have you become so rich all of a sudden that you're scared stiff he might steal all your money? You should be ashamed, Semyon!'

And he turned round again and went right up to the man.

2

After a close look Semyon could see that he was young and healthy. There were no bruises on his body: he was just chilled to the bone and terrified. There he sat, leaning forward without looking at Semyon and apparently too weak to raise his eyes. When Semyon was right next to him he suddenly seemed to wake as if from a trance. He turned his head, opened his eyes and looked straight at Semyon. That one look was enough to allay all Semyon's fears. He threw down the felt boots, undid his belt, laid it over the boots and took off his cloth coat.

'There's no time for talking,' he said. 'Put that on – and be quick about it!'

Then Semyon took the man under the arms and tried to lift him, but he got to his feet without any help. And then

27

Semyon saw that his body was slender and clean, that his legs and arms bore no trace of any wounds; his face was mild and gentle. Semyon threw his coat over his shoulders, but the man could not find the sleeves, so Semyon guided his arms into them, pulled on the coat, wrapped it around him and fastened it with his belt.

Then Semyon took off his tattered cap, intending to put it on the naked man's head, but he felt the cold on his own head and thought, 'I'm completely bald, while he's got long, curly hair.' And he put it back on again. 'It would be better to give him the boots,' he thought.

So he made the man sit down again and put the felt boots on his feet, after which he said, 'There you are, my friend. Stretch your legs a bit and warm yourself. Don't worry, it will all be sorted out later. Now, can you walk?'

The man stood up, looked tenderly at Semyon, but was unable to say one word.

'Why don't you say something? Come on, we can't spend all winter here, we must be on our way. Here, you can lean on my stick if you feel weak. Right, come on!'

And the man started walking – and he walked effortlessly, without lagging behind.

As they went down the road Semyon asked, 'Where are you from?'

'Not from these parts.'

'I thought so – I know everyone round here. But how did you come to be there, by the chapel?'

'I cannot tell you that.'

'Did some men attack you?'

'No, no one harmed me. It was God who punished me.'

'Well, we are all in His hands. All the same, you must have somewhere to go. Where are you heading?'

'Nowhere in particular.'

Semyon was amazed. The man did not strike him as a ruffian, he was so softly spoken, yet he revealed nothing about himself. 'Anything can happen in this world,' Semyon reflected and he told the man, 'All right, come home with me, even if it is a bit out of your way.'

As Semyon walked down the road the stranger did not lag behind for one moment, but kept abreast. The wind got up and the cold air crept under Semyon's shirt. The drink was beginning to wear off and he felt chilled to the marrow.

Sniffling as he went, he wrapped his wife's jacket tighter around himself and thought, 'So much for sheepskins! I go off to buy some and all I do is come home without even the old coat on my back, and with a naked stranger into the bargain! Matryona won't be too pleased about that!' And the thought of his wife depressed him. But the moment he looked at the stranger he remembered the look he had given him at the chapel and his heart filled with joy.

3

Semyon's wife had finished her chores early that day. She had chopped the wood, fetched water, fed the children, had a bite to eat herself and had then sat for a long time wondering when she should bake the bread – that same day or the next. There was still one thick slice left.

'If Semyon has his dinner in the village,' she thought, 'then he won't want much for supper and there'll be enough bread for tomorrow.'

She turned the slice over, 'I shan't do any baking today,' she decided, 'there's only enough flour for one loaf. But we can make this last till Friday.'

So Matryona put the bread away and sat down at the table to patch her husband's shirt. As she worked she thought of him buying the sheepskins for the new winter coat.

'I hope the dealer won't swindle him. He's so simple, that husband of mine. He'd never cheat a soul himself and even a little child could trick him. Eight roubles is a lot of money, enough to buy very good sheepskins. Not the best quality tanned ones perhaps, but still good enough for a nice coat. Last winter was so hard without a proper one! I couldn't even go down to the river, couldn't go anywhere. And when he left this morning he took all the warm clothes we have, leaving me with nothing to wear. Now, he didn't leave all that early. All the same, it's time he was back. I hope my old man hasn't gone drinking!'

These thoughts had just crossed Matryona's mind when the front steps creaked and someone came in. Matryona stuck her needle into the shirt and went out into the hall. There she saw two men – Semyon and someone in felt boots and without a cap.

Matryona immediately smelt the vodka on her husband's breath. 'So, I was right, he's been on the drink,' she thought. And when she saw him standing there, empty-handed and with a guilty grin on his face, wearing nothing but the jacket she had lent him, her heart sank. 'He's gone and spent all that money drinking with some good-for-nothing. What's more, he's got the nerve to bring him home.'

Matryona ushered them in and followed them into the living-room. Now she could see that the stranger was a thin young man and that he was wearing her husband's coat. She could see no shirt under it and he had no cap. Once inside he stood quite still and kept looking down. Matryona concluded that he was a bad lot, as he seemed so nervous.

Frowning, she went over to the stove and waited to see what they would do next.

Semyon took off his cap and sat down on the bench as if he had done no wrong.

'Come on, Matryona, let's have some supper!' he said.

Matryona muttered something to herself and stayed quite still by the stove. She kept looking first at one, then the other, shaking her head. Semyon realized that his wife was annoyed, but there was nothing he could do about it. Pretending not to notice, he took the stranger by the arm.

'Sit down,' he said. 'Let's have something to eat.'

The stranger sat on the bench.

'Well, don't you have anything?'

Matryona lost her temper. 'Yes, I do, but not for you. It seems you've drunk your brains away. You went out to buy some sheepskins and back you come without even the coat you left in. What's more, you bring some half-naked tramp back with you. I don't have any supper for a pair of drunkards like you!'

'Now that's enough of your stupid tongue-wagging, Matryona! You might at least ask who he is.'

'And you can tell me what you did with the money.'

Semyon felt in his pocket, took out the three-rouble note and unfolded it.

'Here it is. Trifonov wouldn't give me any money, but he promised to pay up in a day or so.'

Matryona grew even more furious: in addition to not buying the sheepskins, her husband had lent their only coat to some naked stranger. What's more, he'd brought him back home.

She snatched the note from the table and went off to hide it somewhere.

'I've no supper for you,' she told them. 'You can't expect me to feed every naked drunkard.'

'And you mind your tongue, Matryona. First hear what he has to say . . .'

'What sense will I get from a drunken fool like him? I was right in not wanting to marry an old soak like you! You sold all Mother's linen for drink. And then, instead of buying sheepskins you spend the money on drink.'

Semyon tried hard to make his wife understand that all he had spent on drink was a mere twenty copecks and to explain where he had found the stranger. But she would not let him get a word in edgeways, rattling away nineteen to the dozen and even reminding him of things that had happened ten years ago. On and on she went, until finally she dashed over to Semyon and grabbed his sleeve.

'Give me my jacket back, it's the only one I have and you took it to wear yourself. Give it back, you flea-bitten dog. May you die of a fit!'

Semyon began taking the jacket off and turned a sleeve

inside-out, but his wife tugged so hard that it came apart at
the seams. Then she seized it, threw it over her head and
made for the door. But then she stopped. Her heart seemed
to melt and she felt that she wanted to banish all those spite-
ful feelings and to find out who that man really was.

4

As she stood there, quite still, Matryona said, 'If he were an
honest man he wouldn't be going around without a shirt to
his back. And if you'd been doing what you were supposed
to you'd have told me where you picked up this fine young
fellow!'

'All right, I'll tell you. I was on my way home when I saw
this man sitting by the chapel, naked and frozen. Now, it's
not the kind of weather to go about naked! God must have
led me to him, or he'd have perished. What could I do? Who
knows what may have happened to him? So, I made him
stand up, clothed him and brought him back here. Please
don't be angry, Matryona, it's sinful. Don't forget that we
must all die one day.'

Matryona was about to give him a piece of her mind
again, but then she looked at the stranger and became
silent. There he sat, motionless, on the edge of the bench,
his hands folded on his knees, his head drooping on his
breast. His eyes were closed and he wrinkled his face as
if something were choking him. Matryona still said nothing, but Semyon asked, 'Matryona, is there no love of God
within you?'

At these words Matryona glanced at the stranger and her heart suddenly filled with pity. She came back from the door, went over to the stove, took out the supper, placed a cup on the table, poured out some kvass, brought out the last slice of bread and set out a knife and some spoons. Please eat,' she said.

Semyon nudged the stranger and told him, 'Come and sit at the table.'

Semyon divided the bread into small pieces and they started eating. Matryona sat at one corner of the table, her head on her hand, gazing at the stranger. And she was filled with pity and her heart went out to him. Suddenly, his face brightened, the wrinkles disappeared and he looked up at Matryona and smiled.

After supper Matryona cleared the table and began questioning him.

'Where are you from?'

'Not from these parts.'

'How did you come to be by the wayside?'

'I cannot tell you.'

'Who stole your clothes?'

'God punished me.'

'And you were lying there, all naked?'

'Yes, naked and freezing. And then Semyon saw me and took pity on me. He took off his coat, put it over me and insisted I came home with him. You have given me food and drink and shown compassion. God will reward you!'

Matryona got up, took from the window-sill the old shirt of Semyon's she had been patching and handed it to the stranger. Then she found him some trousers.

'Here, I see you've no shirt, so put this on and lie down where you like – up on the sleeping-bench or over the stove.'

The stranger took off the coat, put on the shirt and trousers and lay on the sleeping-bench. Matryona blew out the candle, took the coat and joined her husband over the stove.

Matryona drew the skirts of the coat over herself and lay down. But she did not fall asleep, for she could not get that stranger out of her mind.

When she remembered that he had eaten their last slice of bread and that they would have none for tomorrow, and that she had given him the shirt and trousers, she became terribly dejected. But then, when she recalled his smile her heart leapt up. For a long time she lay awake and she noticed that Semyon was awake too, as he kept pulling the coat up.

'Semyon!'

'What is it?'

'You two have eaten the last slice of bread and I haven't prepared any more. I don't know what we're going to do tomorrow. Perhaps I can borrow some from our neighbour Malanya.'

'Yes, we'll get by, we won't starve.'

Matryona lay silently for a while and then she said, 'He seems to be a good man, only he doesn't tell us anything about himself.'

'I suppose he can't.'

'Semyon!'

'What?'

'We're always giving, but why does nobody ever give *us* anything?'

Semyon didn't know what to reply. All he said was, 'Let's

talk about that another time,' after which he turned over and went to sleep.

5

Next morning, when Semyon woke up, the children were still asleep and his wife had gone over to the neighbour's to borrow some bread. Only the stranger was sitting on the bench, wearing the old trousers and shirt and looking up. His face was brighter than the evening before. Semyon said, 'Well, my friend. The belly needs food and the body clothes. We all have to earn a living, so what sort of work can you do?'

'I can't do anything.'

Semyon was amazed and replied, 'If a man has the will he can learn anything.'

'Yes, men work for their living, so I'll work too.'

'What's your name?'

'Mikhail.'

'Well, Mikhail, if you don't want to tell us about yourself that's your affair. But we have to earn our living. If you do as I tell you I'll see you have enough to eat.'

'God bless you! I'll learn how to work, just tell me what to do.'

Semyon took a piece of yarn, wound it round his fingers and twisted it.

'It's not hard, just watch . . .'

Mikhail watched and right away he caught the knack, winding the yarn and twisting it just like Semyon.

Then Semyon showed him how to wax it and Mikhail understood at once. Then he showed him how to draw it through and how to stitch. Again Mikhail immediately understood.

Whatever Semyon showed him he mastered right away and within three days was working as if he had been making shoes all his life. He would work without any let-up and ate very little. Only when one job was finished would he stop for a moment and silently look up. He never went out, only spoke when he really had to, and he never joked or laughed.

And in fact the only time they had seen him smile was on that very first evening, when Matryona had given him supper.

6

The days passed, weeks passed, and a year ran its course. Mikhail was still living with Semyon and working for him. The word got round that Semyon's new workman could make boots better and stronger than anyone else. People from all over the district came to Semyon for new boots and he prospered.

One winter's day Semyon and Mikhail were sitting at their work when a three-horse carriage on sleigh runners drove up to the cottage, its bells gaily ringing. When they looked out of the window they saw it had stopped right outside. A boy jumped down from the box and opened the carriage door. A gentleman in a fur coat stepped out, walked up to the front door and climbed the steps. Matryona rushed to fling open the door.

As he came in, the gentleman had to lower his head and then straighten up. But still his head almost touched the ceiling and he filled a whole corner of the room.

Semyon stood up and marvelled at the gentleman: he had never seen anyone like him. Semyon himself was lean, Mikhail was skinny, while Matryona was as thin as a rake. But this visitor seemed like someone from another world: with his full red face and his bull's neck he seemed to be made of cast iron.

He puffed, took off his fur coat, sat on the bench and asked, 'Who is the master bootmaker here?'

Semyon stepped forward and said, 'I am, Your Honour.'

Then the gentleman shouted to his boy, 'Hey, Fedka, bring the leather!'

The boy ran in with a parcel, which the gentleman took and placed on the table.

'Untie it,' he said. The boy untied it.

Then the gentleman pointed at the leather and told Semyon, 'Now, listen to me, bootmaker. Do you see that leather?'

'Yes, I do, Your Honour.'

'Do you know what kind it is?'

Semyon felt it and said, 'It's very good quality.'

'I should say it's good quality! You fool, I bet you've never set eyes on leather like that. It's German and I paid twenty roubles for it.'

Semyon quailed and said, 'Now where would *I* see leather like that?'

'Yes, where indeed! Could you make me a pair of boots out of it?'

'It's possible, Your Honour.'

'I'll give you possible!' the gentleman shouted. 'Now, see you don't forget for whom you're making them and the quality of the leather you'll be using. I want a pair of boots that will last me a year without losing their shape or coming apart at the stitches. If you can do the job, take the leather and cut it up. But if you can't, you'd better tell me here and now. I'm warning you: if the boots split or lose their shape before the year's out I'll have you clapped in prison. But if they keep their shape and don't split for a year I'll pay you ten roubles.'

Semyon was quite afraid and did not know what to reply. He glanced at Mikhail, nudged him with his elbow and whispered, 'Well, shall I take it on?'

Mikhail nodded as if to say, 'Yes, take it on.'

So Semyon followed Mikhail's advice and undertook to make a pair of boots that would not lose their shape or split for a whole year.

Then the gentleman called the boy over to take off his left boot for him and stretched out his leg.

'Take my measurements!'

Semyon sewed together a strip of paper about seventeen inches long, smoothed it out, knelt down, wiped his hands thoroughly on his apron so as not to dirty the gentleman's sock and started measuring. He took the sole and instep measurements. But when he tried to measure the calf he found that the strip of paper was not long enough – the gentleman's calf was as thick as a log.

'Mind you don't make them too tight in the leg,' he said.

Semyon sewed another piece to the strip of paper, while the gentleman sat wriggling his toes in his sock and surveying the people in the room. And then he noticed Mikhail.

'Who's that over there?' he asked.

'He's my master craftsman, he'll be making the boots.'

'Now you watch out,' the gentleman said, 'remember they have to last a whole year.'

When Semyon turned towards Mikhail he saw that he was not even looking at the gentleman, but staring into the corner, as if someone was standing behind him. Mikhail kept staring until suddenly he smiled and his whole face lit up.

'What are you grinning at, idiot?' the gentleman asked. 'You'd better see to it that the boots are ready on time!'

'They'll be ready whenever you want them,' Mikhail replied.

'Good.'

The gentleman put on his boots again, then his fur coat, which he wrapped tightly around him, and went to the door. But he forgot to lower his head and banged it against the lintel. He cursed and rubbed it. Then he climbed into the carriage and drove off.

As soon as he had gone Semyon remarked, 'He's as tough as nails! You couldn't kill him with a mallet. Why, he nearly knocked the lintel out and still he hardly felt a thing!'

'You'd expect him to be strong with the kind of life he leads,' Matryona said. 'Death itself couldn't touch that iron girder!'

'Well, we've taken on the work now,' Semyon told Mikhail, 'and I only hope it doesn't land us in trouble. The leather's very expensive and the gentleman's short-tempered, so we'd better not slip up. Your eyes are sharper than mine and your hands are more skilled, so take the measure and start cutting the leather. I'll sew the vamps later.'

Mikhail obediently took the leather, spread it on the table, folded it in two, took a knife and started cutting.

Matryona went over to watch Mikhail working and was amazed to see what he was doing. Naturally she knew all about boot-making and could see that instead of cutting the leather into the normal shape for boots Mikhail was cutting it into round pieces.

Matryona felt she should point it out, but then she thought, 'Maybe I don't understand how a *gentleman's* boots should be made. Maybe Mikhail knows best, so I won't interfere.'

When he had finished cutting Mikhail took some thread and started sewing the pieces together – not with two ends, as he should have done for boots, but with one end, as if for slippers.

Although Matryona was astonished by this as well, she did not interfere and Mikhail carried on sewing until midday.

When Semyon got up and saw that Mikhail had made a pair of slippers from the gentleman's leather he groaned.

'I don't understand,' he thought, 'how Mikhail, who's

been with me for a whole year without making one mistake, should now go and make such a dreadful mess of things. The gentleman ordered welted high boots and he's made slippers without soles and ruined the leather. How can I face the gentleman now? I can't replace leather of that quality.'

And he told Mikhail, 'What on earth have you done, my friend? You've ruined me! The gentleman ordered high boots and just look what you've made!'

And he was just about to give Mikhail a stern lecture when someone knocked hard on the front door with the iron ring. They looked out of the window and saw that someone had ridden up and was tethering his horse. When the door was opened in came the same young boy who had accompanied the gentleman.

'Good afternoon to you!'

'Good afternoon. What can we do for you?'

'The mistress sent me about those boots.'

'What about them?'

'Just this: the master won't be needing them. He's dead.'

'What did you say?'

'He died in the carriage even before we got home. When we reached the house the others came to help him out, but there he lay, slumped like a sack of potatoes. He was already stiff, stone-dead, and we had a real struggle getting him out. So the mistress told me to come back here. "Tell that shoe-maker," she said, "that the gentleman who called and ordered some boots and left the leather won't be needing them and that instead he must make a pair of soft corpse-slippers as soon as he can." She told me to wait until they're ready. So here I am.'

Mikhail collected the offcuts from the table and rolled them up. Then he took the soft slippers he had already made, slapped them together, wiped them with his apron and handed them to the boy, who took them.

'Goodbye, masters! Good luck to you!' he said as he left.

8

Another year passed, then another, until Mikhail was in his sixth year with Semyon. He lived just as before, never going out, speaking only when he had to. And all that time he smiled only twice – when the old woman had first given him supper and then when the rich gentleman called. Semyon thought the world of his workman and no longer inquired where he was from. His only fear was that Mikhail might leave him.

One day they were all at home and Matryona was putting iron pots into the oven, while the children were scampering along the benches and looking out of the windows. Semyon was stitching at one window, while Mikhail was heeling a boot at the other.

One of the little boys ran along the bench to Mikhail, leant on his shoulder and looked through the window.

'Look, Uncle Mikhail! There's a lady with two little girls. I think she's coming here. One of the girls is limping.'

When the boy said this, Mikhail put down his work, turned to the window and looked out into the street.

Semyon was amazed: Mikhail had never looked out into the street before, but now he was glued to the window and staring at something. Semyon, too, looked out and saw that a well-dressed woman with two little girls in fur coats and thick woollen shawls were in fact coming towards the cottage. The girls were so alike it would have been impossible to tell them apart were it not that one had a crippled left leg and walked with a limp.

The woman climbed the steps, fumbled for the latch and opened the door. She let the little girls in first and then followed them.

'Good day, everyone!' she said.

'Welcome! What can we do for you?'

The woman sat at the table while the girls, feeling shy with all those people in the room, snuggled against her knees.

'I'd like some leather shoes for the girls, for the spring,' she said.

'That's no problem. Although we've never made such small ones before we can do them – either welted or lined with linen. This is Mikhail, my master shoemaker.'

Semyon turned to Mikhail and saw that he had stopped working and was sitting there with his eyes fixed on the little girls.

Semyon was quite surprised. True, the girls were very pretty – plump, with black eyes and rosy little cheeks – and wore fine fur coats and shawls. Still, he could not understand why Mikhail should be staring like that, as if he knew them.

Semyon kept wondering and then started discussing the price with the woman. This was finally agreed and Semyon took his measure. The woman lifted the lame girl on to one knee and said, 'Measure her twice and make one shoe for her lame foot and three for the sound one: they take exactly the same size, because they're twins.'

Semyon took the measurements and inquired about the little lame girl.

'What happened? Such a pretty little girl. Was she born like that?'

'No, she was crushed by her mother.'

Just then Matryona joined in. She was wondering who the woman was and whose children they were.

'You're their mother, aren't you?'

'No, dear woman, I'm not their mother, nor am I a relative. They were complete strangers and I adopted them.'

'They're not your own and yet you seem so fond of them!'

'How can I help being fond of them? I breast-fed them both. I did have a child of my own once, but it pleased God to take him. I didn't love him as much as these little girls, though.'

'So whose are they?'

9

And the woman proceeded to tell them the whole story.

'It all started about six years ago, when these little girls lost their father and mother the same week – the father was buried on the Tuesday and the mother died on the Friday. So, for three days they had no father and on the fourth they lost their mother. At that time my husband and I were farm-workers and our yard was right next door. The father was a lone wolf and worked as a woodcutter. One day when they were cutting down some trees they let one fall right on him and it crushed his insides. They had hardly got him back to the village when his soul went up to heaven and the same week his widow gave birth to twins – these little girls. She was a poor woman, all on her own, with no other women, young or old, to help her. Alone she gave birth and alone she died.

'The next morning I went to see how she was, but the poor thing was already stiff and cold. When she died she'd rolled over on to this little girl and twisted her leg out of shape. Then the villagers came, washed the body and laid it out. Then they made a coffin and buried her. Good folk they were. So the two little girls were left alone in the world, and who was going to look after them? I happened to be the only woman in that village who'd had a baby at the time and I'd been breast-feeding my first-born for about eight weeks. So I took care of the girls for the time being. The men thought hard about what to do with the orphans and in the end they told me, "You'd better look after them for now, Marya, until we manage to sort something out." So I breast-fed the girl who hadn't been harmed, but not the one who'd been crippled, as I didn't expect her to live. And then I thought to myself, "Why should that little angel be left to fade away?" I took pity on her too and started feeding her, so that in the end I was feeding all three of them – my own first-born and these two, at my own breasts! I was young, strong and well-nourished and God gave me so much milk that it filled my breasts to overflowing. Sometimes I'd feed two at a time, with the third waiting, and when one had had its fill, I'd put the third to my breast. But it was God's will that I should nurse these little girls and bury my own child before he was two years old. And God never gave me another one. But after that I became quite well off. My second husband's working for a corn merchant and we live at the mill. He earns good money and we live well. But as we've no children of our own I'd be terribly lonely without these two little girls. How can I help loving them? They are the apple of my eye!'

The woman pressed the lame girl to her with one hand and wiped the tears from her cheeks with the other.

Matryona sighed. 'There's a lot of truth in the saying "You can live without mother or father, but you can't live without God."'

They chatted together for a while and then the woman got up to leave. Semyon and his wife saw them out and then they looked at Mikhail: he was sitting there, his arms folded on his knees, and he was looking up and smiling.

10

Semyon went over to Mikhail and asked, 'What is it?'

Mikhail rose from the bench, put down his work, took off his apron, bowed to Semyon and Matryona and said, 'Please forgive me, you good people. God has forgiven me, so please forgive me too.'

And the shoemaker and his wife saw a light shining from Mikhail. And Semyon stood up, bowed in turn and said, 'I can see you are no ordinary mortal and I cannot detain you any longer or question you. But please tell me one thing: why were you so miserable when I first found you and brought you home? And why, when my wife gave you supper, did you smile and from that time onwards brighten up?

And why, when that rich gentleman ordered those boots, did you smile again and become even more cheerful? And why, when that woman brought those little girls here just now, did you smile a third time and become the very picture of joy? Please tell me, Mikhail. What is that light coming from you and why did you smile three times?'

'The light is radiating from me,' Mikhail replied, 'because I had been punished, but now God has forgiven me. And I smiled three times because I was commanded to discover three truths and I have discovered them. I discovered the first truth when your wife took pity on me – that is why I smiled for the first time. The second truth I discovered when that rich gentleman ordered the boots – and then I smiled again. And just now, when I saw those two little girls, I discovered the last of the three truths – and I smiled for the third time.'

'Tell me, Mikhail,' Semyon asked, 'why did God punish you and what are those three truths, so that I too may know them?'

Mikhail replied, 'God punished me because I disobeyed Him. I was an angel of the Lord and I disobeyed Him. Yes, I was an angel in heaven and the Lord sent me down to earth to take a woman's soul. I flew down and saw the woman lying there. She was sick, all alone and had just given birth to twins, two little girls. There they were, crawling around their mother, but she was unable to put them to her breasts. When she saw me she understood that God had sent me to take her soul. She burst into tears and said, "Angel of the Lord! My husband has just been buried, killed by a falling tree. I have no sister, no aunt, no grandmother – no one to bring up my little orphans. So please don't take my soul, let me suckle my babies, bring them up and set them on their feet. Children cannot live without father or mother!" And I did what she asked, pressed one little girl to her breast, put the other in her arms and ascended to heaven. I flew to God and told Him, "I could not bring myself to take the soul of a woman who had just borne twins. The father was killed by a falling tree and the mother had just given birth and begged me not to take her soul. 'Let me suckle my children, bring them up and set them on their feet. Children cannot live without a father or mother,' she pleaded. So I did not take that woman's soul." And then God said, "If you go down to earth and take that woman's soul you will discover three truths: you will learn *what dwells in man, what is not given to man* and *what men live by*. When you have learnt these truths you shall return to heaven." So I flew down to earth again and took the mother's soul. The babies dropped from her breasts and her body rolled over on to one of them, crushing its leg. Then I rose above the village, wishing to return her soul to God, but I was seized by a strong wind and my wings drooped and fell off. And so the soul alone returned to God and I fell to earth, by the roadside.'

11

And now Semyon and Matryona realized whom they had been clothing and feeding and had taken in to live with them. And they both wept for joy and fear. And the angel said, 'I was alone and naked in that field. Never before had

I known the needs of man, never had I known cold or hunger. But now I was an ordinary mortal, cold and hungry and not knowing what to do. And then I saw a chapel in the field, built for the glory of God. So I went to it to seek shelter. But it was locked and I could not enter. So I sat down behind it to shelter from the wind. Evening came and I was famished, freezing and in pain. Suddenly I heard a man coming down the road. He was carrying a pair of boots and talking to himself. For the first time since I became a man I saw the mortal face of man. It terrified me and I turned away. And I could hear this man wondering how to protect his body from the winter cold and feed his wife and children. And I thought, "I am perishing with cold and hunger, but here is someone whose only thought is how to find a warm coat for himself and his wife, and food for his family. I cannot expect any help from him." When the man saw me he frowned, looking even more terrifying, and he passed me by. I was desperate. But suddenly I heard him coming back. As I looked he no longer seemed the same man. Before, his face had borne the stamp of death, but now he had suddenly become alive again and in that face I could see God. He came up to me, clothed me and took me to his home. When we arrived a woman came out to meet us and she spoke. This woman was even more terrifying than the man. Her breath seemed to come from the grave and I was almost choked by that deathly stench. She wished to cast me out into the cold and I knew that if she did that she would die. Then suddenly her husband told her to think of God and at once she was transformed. When she had given us supper I returned the look she gave me and saw that death no longer dwelt in her, but life. And in her too I could see God.

'And I recalled God's first lesson: *thou shalt learn what dwelleth in man*. And now I knew that it is Love that dwells in man. I was overjoyed that God had begun to reveal what He had promised to reveal, and I smiled for the first time. But I did not know the whole truth yet. I did not yet know what is not given to man and what men live by.

'And so I came to live with you and one year passed. One day a rich gentleman came to order a pair of boots that would last a year without splitting or losing their shape. When I looked at him I suddenly saw my comrade, the Angel of Death, standing behind him. No one but I could see that angel. And I knew that he would take the gentleman's soul before sunset. And I thought, "Here is a man who wants to provide for himself for a year from now but does not know that by evening he will be dead.' And so I remembered God's second lesson: *thou shalt learn what is* not *given to man*.

'What dwells in man I already knew. Now I knew that which is not given to man: it is not given to him to know his bodily needs. And I smiled for the second time. I rejoiced that I had seen my fellow angel and that God had revealed His second truth.

'But still I did not know everything. I did not understand what it is that men live by. And so I lived on, waiting for God to reveal this last truth to me. In my sixth year that woman came here with the two little girls. I recognized the girls and learnt how they had stayed alive. After this discovery I thought, "The mother pleaded with me for her children's sake and I believed what she said, thinking that children cannot live without father or mother. But the other woman had nursed them and brought them up." And when I saw how much love this woman had for the children and how she wept over them I saw the living God in her and understood *what men live by*. And I realized that God had revealed His last lesson and had forgiven me. So I smiled for the third time.'

12

And the angel's body was bared and it was robed in light, so that the eye could not look upon it. And the angel's voice grew louder, as though it came not from him, but from heaven itself. And the angel said, 'I have learned that men live not by selfishness, but by love.

'It was not given to the mother to know what her children needed for their lives. Nor was it given to the rich man to know what his true needs were. Nor is it given to any man to know, before the sun has set, whether he will need boots for his living body or slippers for his corpse. When I became a mortal I survived not by thinking of myself, but through the love that dwelt in a passer-by and his wife, and the compassion and love they showed me. The two orphans' lives were preserved, not by what others may have intended for them, but by the love that dwelt in the heart of a woman, a complete stranger, and by the love and compassion she showed them. Indeed, all men live not by what they may intend for their own well-being, but by the love that dwells in others.

'Previously I had known that God gave life to men and desired that they should live. But then I came to know something else.

'I came to understand that God does not wish men to live apart and that is why He does not reveal to each man what he needs for himself *alone*. On the contrary, He wishes men to live in peace and harmony with each other and for this reason He has revealed to each and every one of them what *all* men need, as well as themselves.

'And I understood that men only think that they live by caring only about themselves: in reality they live by love alone. He who dwells in love dwells in God, and God in him, for God is love.'

And the angel sang the Lord's praises and the hut shook with the sound of his voice. And the roof parted and a pillar of fire rose from earth to heaven. Semyon and his wife and children prostrated themselves; the angel's wings unfurled and he soared into the sky.

When Semyon came to his senses the hut was just as it had always been and there was no one there but him and his family.